"Alex, are you crazy!" Janie exclaimed. "You mean you really want to take your mother's frozen turkey to Sunday school?"

"Sure," Alex replied.

"But don't you think your mother might miss the turkey?" asked Janie.

"Well, maybe," Alex admitted. "But there are so many other things in the freezer, that maybe she might forget about it."

"I dunno, Alex. I don't think you better do it."

"Aw, come on, Janie," Alex pleaded. "We can't let the boys win the Easter basket contest. If they win, Joshua Barton will never let us forget it!"

"Well, since you put it that way . . . "

The ALEX Series
by Nancy Simpson Levene

ALEX

Grapefruit Basket Upset

Nancy Simpson Levene

Chariot Books™

To my Father in heaven,
who lovingly calls His children to walk with Him,
and to Sally Jadlow,
who has walked the extra mile
for Cara and me.

Chariot Books™ is an imprint of
David C. Cook Publishing Co.
David C. Cook Publishing Co., Elgin, Illinois 60120
David C. Cook Publishing Co., Weston, Ontario
Nova Distribution Ltd., Newton Abbot, England

GRAPEFRUIT BASKET UPSET
© 1991 by Nancy R. Simpson for text and GraphCom
Corporation for interior illustrations.

Cover design by Bill Paetzold
Cover illustration by Neal Hughes

Printed in the United States of America

ISBN 1-55513-768-7

CONTENTS

. . . And what does the Lord require of you
But to do justice, to love kindness,
And to walk humbly with your God?

Micah 6:8
New American Standard Bible

. . . let us strip off anything that slows us down or
holds us back, and especially those sins that wrap
themselves so tightly around our feet and trip us up;
and let us run with patience the particular race that
God has set before us.

Hebrews 12:1
The Living Bible

ACKNOWLEDGMENTS

I would like to thank Reverend R. Charles Spivey for letting me use some ideas from his sermon "Walking With God." I also thank my daughter, Cara, for laughing with me over this book before it was ever written.

CHAPTER 1

To the Rescue

"Alex! Come quick! The most awesome thing has happened!" shouted the young, freckle-faced boy. He stood on the front porch and hopped impatiently from one foot to the other.

"Huh? What are you talking about, Jason?" Alex replied. She stared with annoyance at her younger neighbor. When the doorbell had blasted several times in a row, Mother had asked Alex to answer the door before the family went deaf from the noise. Alex had been enjoying a tall stack of pancakes covered with the most wonderful, drippy, blueberry syrup.

Alex glared at Jason. He had better

have a good excuse for pulling her away from her Sunday breakfast.

As it turned out, Jason did have a good excuse. In fact, what Jason said next made Alex forget all about her pancakes and drippy syrup.

"Miss Muff just had her kittens! She had four of them!" Jason cried with excitement.

"Brussels sprouts! Rudy, come quick!" Alex shouted, running to the kitchen to get her younger brother. Halfway there, she remembered she had left Jason on the front porch.

Running back to the front door, Alex dragged Jason inside. They both ran to the kitchen.

"Whoa! Slow down!" protested Father, whose coffee cup rattled alarmingly. "What's going on here? An earthquake?"

"No," Jason laughed at Father's question. "Miss Muff just had her kittens!" he announced proudly.

"Really?" Eight-year-old Rudy bounded

out of his chair. "I wanna go see 'em!"

"Me, too!" Alex agreed.

Even Barbara, Alex's older sister, looked interested. She, however, was fifteen years old and too sensible to leave her breakfast half finished.

Mother threw up her hands. She knew it was no use trying to get Alex and Rudy to finish their breakfasts. "You can go see the kittens," Mother told them, "but be back soon. We need to get ready for church."

Alex, Rudy, and Jason hurried as fast as they could across the yard to Jason's house next door. The children were excited. They had been waiting so long for Miss Muff to have her very first litter of kittens.

Rushing through the front door, Jason led the way to his parents' bedroom.

"You mean the kittens are in here?" Alex asked in surprise. She and Rudy followed Jason past his parents' bed, around his mother's dresser, and into

the bathroom that was connected to the
bedroom.

"Here they are!" Jason announced.
He dropped to the bathroom floor and
opened a cabinet door under the sink.

Alex and Rudy peered into the shad-
owy area. They could just barely see the
faint outlines of a box. From inside the
box, two bright, yellow eyes stared back
at them.

"It's too dark," Rudy complained. "I
can't see the kittens."

10

"We have to use a flashlight," Jason replied. He reached inside the cabinet and pulled out a flashlight. Switching it on, he flashed its beam into the box.

"Oh!" Alex and Rudy gasped. Four tiny bundles snuggled tightly against Miss Muff's calico fur. They were so little that Alex thought they looked more like baby mice than kittens.

"Why do you keep 'em under the sink?" Rudy asked.

Jason laughed. "Because that's where Miss Muff picked to have her babies. And my mom says you don't argue with a mother cat who's about to have kittens."

"But why would she pick such a small, dark place?" wondered Alex.

"Oh, she likes it that way," Jason told Alex. "Mom says she feels safe in such an out-of-the-way place. Besides, you know how good cats can see in the dark. In a few days," Jason went on, "we're going to try to move her and the kittens to a different place. Dad says he doesn't want to share his bathroom with a litter of kittens for eight weeks!"

Alex and Rudy laughed. Jason's father was the pastor of their church. It was funny to imagine kittens attacking Reverend Peterson's toes as he got ready to take a shower!

Suddenly grown-up voices sounded outside the bathroom door. Alex looked up to see her mother and father enter the bathroom. Jason's parents were right behind them.

"Of course we had to come and see the kittens," Alex's father was saying. "After all, it is the most important event that has happened in the neighborhood for a long time."

"Oh, yes," Jason's father agreed. "And naturally, it had to occur in my bathroom!"

Everyone laughed. Mother and Father squeezed to the floor beside Alex and Rudy and peeked at the kittens in the box under the sink. Miss Muff meowed politely. She seemed proud to show off her kittens to so much company.

"Can we get a kitten?" Alex asked her parents hopefully.

"With our monster of a dog?" Mother exclaimed. "I'd be afraid he might hurt a little kitten."

"No, he wouldn't! One time Dan brought over his kitten and T-Bone didn't hurt it," Alex reminded her mother. Dan was another neighborhood friend.

"Yes, but T-Bone scared all of us by picking the kitten up in his teeth!" replied Mother.

"He picked it up by the scruff of the neck just the way a mother cat would," said Alex. "Don't you remember? You said it was very smart of T-Bone to know how to do that."

"I remember," Mother smiled. "I still wonder how that dog knew how to pick up a kitten that way."

"He's a very smart dog," declared

Alex. "Can we get a kitten?" she asked again.

"We'll see," was the only reply that she received.

Later that morning, as the family rode to church, Alex asked Barbara, "Why didn't you come over and see Jason's kittens?"

"I wanted to," Barbara admitted, "but I had to wash my hair and do my nails before church."

Alex rolled her eyes upward and heaved a silent sigh. Her sister tried always to look like a model right out of a magazine. She could not appear outside the house without just the right shade of lipstick and nail polish.

"Well, you ought to see the kittens," Alex told her sister. She spoke loud enough for her parents to hear. "They are so cute. Don't you think the kittens are cute, Mom?"

"Yes, Alex," Mother said with a smile.

"Did you like the kittens, Dad?" Alex

leaned over the front seat to talk to her father.

"I did, indeed, Firecracker," Father boomed, using her nickname. "But that does not mean we want to keep one of Jason's kittens," he added with a wink at Mother.

"Oh, Dad!" Alex exclaimed. She bounced back in her seat, upset that her father had guessed why she was asking him about the kittens.

"Now, Alex," Mother said gently, "your father and I have not decided whether we want to get a kitten right now. You will just have to wait until we make a decision."

"Okay," Alex sighed. She stared out of the window as they continued their ride to church. "Please, Lord Jesus," she prayed silently, "help me to get a kitten."

As soon as Alex got to church, she hurried to tell her best friend, Janie, all about the kittens. She found Janie in the fifth-grade Sunday school classroom.

Other boys and girls were there, too. Their teacher, Mrs. Winthrop, had not yet arrived.

"Oh! I want to see the kittens!" Janie exclaimed as soon as she heard the news. "I bet they are so cute!"

"Oh! I bet they are so cute!" echoed a teasing voice behind the girls.

Alex and Janie whirled around. Joshua Barton stood directly behind them. His hands were clasped to his chest and his eyelashes batted at the ceiling.

"Go away, Joshua!" Janie cried angrily.

"Yeah, leave us alone!" Alex demanded.

"Leave us alone!" Joshua echoed in a shrill voice. He made a face at Alex. Some of the other boys laughed. They joined in on the teasing. Suddenly, one of the boys grabbed Janie's purse off her shoulder.

"Give me back my purse!" Janie hollered.

The boys only laughed and playfully

tossed the purse to each other. Alex and Janie lunged this way and that way for the purse, but they could not get it.

In the scramble, one boy threw the purse too high in the air, and it landed KERPLOP! on the top of a stack of boxes on a tall filing cabinet.

"Oh, no!" Janie wailed. "I'll never get my purse now."

The boys laughed and congratulated themselves on getting the purse stuck in such an impossibly high place.

"Alex, what am I going to do?" Janie cried in despair.

"Brussels sprouts," Alex sighed. It looked like it was up to her to rescue the purse. She pulled a stool over to the filing cabinet and, climbing on top of it, managed to pull herself up on top of the cabinet. Balancing carefully, Alex slowly raised to a standing position.

"Alex, be careful!" Janie pleaded.

"Uh, don't worry, Janie," Alex replied. She tried to sound confident in front of the boys. Actually, from where Alex stood, it looked like a long way to the ground. To make matters worse, the filing cabinet was narrow and rather slippery. It also felt a bit wobbly.

Feeling somewhat dizzy, Alex turned to the stack of boxes on the cabinet. Reaching into the top one, Alex pulled out Janie's purse.

"YEA!" The girls clapped.

Alex took a bow and then threw the purse down to Janie. Janie held on to it tightly, taking no chances that it would be stolen again.

"So you think you're pretty smart, huh?" a boy hollered up at Alex. "Let's see ya get down now." With that, he moved the stool away from the filing cabinet.

"Hey! Put it back!" Alex yelled. For a moment, she forgot where she was and angrily stomped her foot down hard. The sudden movement made the cabinet shake back and forth. Boxes began to slide off its top.

"Oh, no!" Alex groaned as crayons, scissors, and glue fell out of the boxes as they crashed to the floor.

Almost immediately, Mrs. Winthrop hurried through the door. She was followed by teachers from nearby class-rooms who had heard the loud crash and wondered what had happened.

Alex, on her hands and knees on top of the filing cabinet, looked down at the group of teachers. They all stared up at her.

"Uh, hi," she weakly smiled.

CHAPTER 2

Flying Fruit

"Alex!" Mrs. Winthrop exclaimed. "What are you doing up there on the filing cabinet?"

"Uh, well, I was getting Janie's purse," Alex began to explain. She knew that her face was bright red with embarrassment. She was going to get those boys for this!

Someone pushed the stool back by the filing cabinet and a teacher helped Alex climb down. Alex and the other girls told Mrs. Winthrop what had happened. Mrs. Winthrop made the boys apologize to Alex and Janie. She also made them pick up the craft items that had spilled and put them back in the boxes.

When things had quieted down, Mrs. Winthrop announced, "We are going to have a contest!"

Alex looked up eagerly. She loved to compete at sports, mostly softball and soccer. She had a feeling, however, that Mrs. Winthrop meant a different kind of contest.

"The contest will be between the boys and the girls," said the Sunday school teacher. She held up two very large baskets. One had a pink ribbon tied to its handle. The other had a blue ribbon.

"We are going to see which group can fill their Easter basket with the most canned goods," explained Mrs. Winthrop.

"The girls will win, of course," Alex said loudly.

"No way! The boys will win!" shouted one of the boys.

Mrs. Winthrop held up her hand. "We will collect the food on Palm Sunday. Then we will distribute it to poor families before Easter. That gives you only seven weeks to bring your cans of food. Be sure to ask your parents to buy extra canned food."

"I need to bring cans of food to Sunday school next week," Alex said to her mother when they got home from church. She told Mother how the boys and the girls in her class were going to compete to see who could bring the most food to fill their Easter baskets.

"Sounds very exciting," Mother smiled.

"May I have some cans of food now?" Alex asked. "I need to start counting how many Janie and I can bring."

"Well, let's see," Mother opened a cupboard in the kitchen. "I guess I could let you have my extra can of mushroom soup."

Alex wrinkled her nose. Who would want mushroom soup for Easter? "Don't you have any extra green beans or something?" she asked her mother.

"No, that's all I can give you for now,"

replied Mother. "When I go to the grocery store next week, I'll buy you a couple of extra cans."

"A couple?" Alex complained. "That's not very much. I'll need a lot more to beat the boys."

"Now, Alex," Mother frowned, "you cannot expect to fill the entire Easter basket yourself. The other girls will have to bring their cans, too."

"I know," said Alex. "But I want to bring more than just a couple of cans."

"We'll buy two extra cans at the store this week and two extra next week. That's four cans plus the mushroom soup, making five cans altogether. I think that's plenty for one person to bring," Mother told Alex.

"Okay," Alex said in a low voice. She stomped upstairs to her bedroom and flopped on the bed. Five cans was not nearly enough cans even to begin to fill that giant Easter basket! What if the other girls didn't bring any cans? The boys would win easily. She had to find a way to get more cans of food. But how?

The next week at school, Alex had to put up with teasing from the boys.

"Been climbing any more filing cabinets, Alex?" Joshua Barton yelled loudly.

Before Alex could stop him, Joshua made sure that everyone in their fifth grade classroom heard how Alex had been stuck on top of the filing cabinet.

"Well, I could have got down easy," Alex retorted, "but somebody moved the stool."

That remark made her classmates laugh even harder. Even Mrs. Hibbits, their teacher, smiled.

Later, at lunch time, Alex and her friends, Janie, Lorraine, and Julie, complained about Joshua Barton and his constant teasing.

"He told the whole class that I climbed on top of the filing cabinet at Sunday school," Alex moaned. "I was so embarrassed!"

"That Joshua Barton is a total pest!" Janie declared.

"Yeah, and I sure don't want him and the other boys to win the Easter basket contest," added Alex.

"If the boys win, we'd never hear the end of it from Joshua," Janie agreed.

"What are you talking about?" Lorraine and Julie asked. Alex and Janie told their friends about the contest between the boys and the girls to fill Easter baskets with canned goods.

"My mom's only going to give me five cans to take to Sunday school," Alex said glumly. "How about you, Janie? How many cans can you bring?"

"Probably only three or four," Janie answered.

"That's not enough!" Alex banged her fist on the table. "We need more cans."

"Yeah, but how are we going to get them?" Janie asked.

"I don't know," Alex admitted. "Does anybody have an idea?" she asked her friends.

"Not me," Janie answered.

"Not me," replied both Julie and Lorraine.

"And not me," Alex added with a big sigh.

"This is why I usually like to go to the grocery store by myself," Mother grumbled in a half-teasing manner. She waited while Rudy positioned himself on the back of the grocery cart. Every time Mother stopped to pick an item off the shelf, she had to be careful not to let go of the cart. Otherwise, Rudy's weight would tip the cart over backwards.

"You are really much too big to ride on the grocery cart, Rudy," Mother told him.

"But it's fun!" Rudy replied.

Mother sighed and rolled the cart past the stacked bags of potatoes and the bin

full of onions. She stopped in front of a
giant mound of apples.

"Looks like a new shipment," Mother
commented more to herself than to Alex
and Rudy. She began to pick apples out
of the mound.

Rudy hopped off the cart and strolled
down the center of the aisle. It was lined
on either side with fruits and vegetables.
He stopped by a bin full of big, yellow
grapefruit.

Alex stayed near her mother and the

apples. She almost wished she hadn't come to the grocery store. It was not too exciting to watch her mother dig through a stack of apples and then move on to the oranges. Alex sighed. It had taken her mother a whole week before she had brought Alex to the grocery store to select canned goods for her Sunday school's Easter basket. Mother said she had forgotten all about it last week. How could her mother have forgotten something so important?

Looking up, Alex was startled to see a large, yellow object flying through the air and heading straight for her. It was a big grapefruit! Putting up her hands, Alex caught the grapefruit a moment before it hit her face.

"Ha, ha, ha!" Rudy laughed out loud from the other end of the fruit and vegetable aisle.

"Very funny!" Alex called to her brother. She stepped a few feet away from the apple counter and, after making sure that Mother was not watching, fired the grapefruit back at her brother.

Rudy just barely managed to catch the big fruit before it splattered to the floor. Then, hopping backwards on one foot and pretending to be a professional quarterback, Rudy threw the grapefruit in a long, powerful pass back up the aisle.

The grapefruit sailed over the piles of fruit and vegetables in a high arc. Alex went out for the pass, keeping her eyes on the flying fruit. She backed farther and farther up the aisle. Leaping into the air for the catch, Alex suddenly heard her mother yell, "ALEX! WHAT ARE YOU DOING?" The sudden cry caused Alex to lose her balance. She missed the grapefruit but found herself crashing backwards into the mound of shiny red apples.

CHAPTER 3

Grocery Store Disaster

CRASH! WHOMP! THUD! Apples flew everywhere as Alex fell backwards into the giant mound. Falling far down into the wooden bin, Alex became stuck, her feet and legs waving frantically in the air.

"Help! Help!" she cried.

Mother ran to pull her out. "Are you all right?" she asked Alex.

"Yeah, I guess so," Alex replied. With Mother's help, she climbed out of the apple bin and stared around her in dismay. What a disaster! The wooden bin was tilted lopsided. Most of the apples had fallen out of it. The floor of the grocery store looked like a sea of red apples. They had lodged under grocery carts and people's feet. Nobody could move! The apples had blocked the carts from rolling anywhere.

"WHAT HAPPENED? WHO DID THIS?" The store manager suddenly appeared and ran to the scene.

"Uh, I'm very sorry," Mother apologized to the store manager. "It seems that my daughter fell into your apple bin."

"How in the world did she do that?" the store manager exclaimed.

"That's what I'd like to know," Mother replied. She looked straight at Alex for an answer.

"Uh, well, ummmm . . . " Alex stalled. She didn't know how to tell Mother and the angry store manager that she and Rudy had been throwing a grapefruit back and forth.

"She was trying to catch this grapefruit!" said a shrill voice behind Alex.

Alex, Mother, and the store manager turned to see an older woman staring at them with a very unhappy frown on her face. She pointed down at her grocery cart. Inside the cart was a cake, or what used to be a cake. It now looked more like a squishy mess. On top of it sat a large, yellow grapefruit.

"It was going to be my husband's birthday cake," the older woman sighed.

"Oh, no!" Alex gasped. "You mean the grapefruit landed on top of your cake?"

The older woman nodded.

"Wait a minute," Mother suddenly demanded. "Let me get this straight. Were you and Rudy playing catch with a grapefruit?"

"Yes," Alex admitted. "I was trying to catch it when I crashed into the apples. I'm really sorry."

For a few moments, Mother looked as if she did not know what to say. Finally, she demanded, "Rudy come over here!"

Rudy slowly shuffled over to where

Mother and Alex were standing. Alex could tell by the bright red tips of his ears that he was just as embarrassed as she was.

"Alex and Rudy," Mother said, "You owe the store manager an apology for spilling apples all over the floor."

Alex and Rudy apologized to the store manager.

"You also owe this lady an apology for squashing her cake with a grapefruit," Mother told them.

Alex and Rudy apologized to the woman.

"I will buy you another cake," Mother promised the older woman.

Alex, Rudy, and Mother helped the store manager and his assistants pick up the apples from the floor. They piled them all in one big box.

"I am very sorry that this happened and I will pay for the damaged apples," Mother offered the store manager.

"Oh, don't worry about it," the store manager replied. He seemed to be in a much better mood after the apples had been picked up. "Just don't use my grape-fruit for a football any more," he told Alex and Rudy.

"We won't," Alex and Rudy promised. They followed Mother across the store to the bakery department. There Mother bought another birthday cake for the older woman.

"I have never been so embarrassed!" Mother said to Alex and Rudy once they were alone. "What made you do such a thing?"

"Well," Alex tried to think of an answer, "it seemed like fun. . . ."

"And everything was OK until I threw the grapefruit too high," Rudy added.

"Yeah," Alex frowned at her brother. "If you would have thrown it right, everything would have been okay."

"No, everything would not have been okay," said Mother. "It was wrong to throw the grapefruit. You know you should not throw anything in the grocery store. You ended up ruining a birthday cake and a whole bin of apples."

"We're sorry." Alex and Rudy hung their heads.

"Your father and I are trying not only to teach you to know the difference between right and wrong, but also to be responsible enough to choose to do the right thing," said Mother.

"I guess we chose to do the wrong thing this time," Alex sighed.

"I guess you did," Mother agreed.

At the lunch table the following day, Alex told her friends about the apple disaster at the grocery store.

"You mean all of the apples spilled to the floor?" Janie asked in amazement.

"All of them," Alex nodded.

"And they rolled under everybody's grocery carts?" Lorraine exclaimed with a giggle.

"Yep," Alex replied without cracking a smile.

"And the grapefruit squished a lady's cake?" Julie laughed out loud. So did all the other girls.

When they had quieted down again, Alex said, "Mom is making me and Rudy pay for the cake out of our allowances."

"Did you get any canned goods for the Easter basket at church?" Janie wanted to know.

"No," Alex frowned. "I didn't want to ask my mom to buy me any cans after

Rudy and I had caused so much trouble." She held her head in her hands. "The way things are going, I may never get to bring any cans to Sunday school."

"Well, what are we going to do?" Janie persisted. "I heard Joshua Barton say that he was going to bring a dozen cans next Sunday for the boys' Easter basket."

"A dozen cans!" Alex whistled. "Where'd he get that many?"

"He said his mom found them on sale," Janie replied.

Alex frowned. She thought for a moment. Suddenly, her face brightened. "Well, I guess it's time to start our campaign."

"Huh?" her friends stared at her. "What do you mean?"

"Oh, you know," Alex waved her hand. "Whenever somebody wants to get elected to mayor or something, they go out and knock on doors and ask people to vote for them. They campaign for votes. Well, we are going to campaign for food!"

"You mean we're going to knock on people's doors and ask them for green beans?" Janie asked wide-eyed.

The others laughed.

"That's exactly what I mean," Alex told Janie. "We'll tell them that our church is collecting cans of food for poor people and ask them if they have any spare cans to give us."

"That's a good idea!" Julie chimed in. "Lorraine and I will help you. We can go all over the neighborhood. We'll get lots of cans!"

"Oh, this is exciting!" Janie clapped her hands. "Wait 'til old Joshua Barton sees how many cans we drop into the girls' Easter basket."

"Yeah, his twelve cans will look like chicken feed," Lorraine remarked.

The girls laughed.

"So, when do we start?" Julie asked Alex.

"We gotta wait until next week," Alex said sourly. "I'm grounded for the rest of this week."

"Then we'll do it first thing after school on Monday," her friends replied.

"Okay! That will be great!" agreed Alex.

Alex hated to keep secrets from her mother. She always felt sneaky when she tried to hide something, but this time she felt that it was necessary.

"It's not like I think we're doing anything wrong. . . . " She tried to explain her feelings to Janie on the way home from school the following Monday. "After all, we are going to tell the neighbors that we are collecting cans of food for our church's Easter basket."

"Right," Janie interrupted. "So why don't you want to tell your mom that we are going to ask the neighbors for food?"

"Well," Alex said thoughtfully, "after all the trouble at the grocery store last week, I'd rather not mention anything about food to my mom. I mean, it would just remind her all over again of what Rudy and I did."

The girls continued their walk home. They had barely reached Alex's house when Julie and Lorraine rang the front doorbell.

Mother answered the door. "Why, hello. What are you girls up to?"

"Uh, nothing," Alex answered before her friends could say a word. "They just came over to play with me and Janie. Come on, let's go outside." She hurried her friends out the door.

"Alex!" Mother called after them. "Don't go very far!"

"Oh, we won't," Alex answered. "We'll just be around the neighborhood."

"She's probably afraid we'll go to the shopping mall again," Julie giggled as soon as Mother had shut the door. Once, a few months ago, Alex, Janie, Julie, and Lorraine had become lost while taking

Alex's dog, T-Bone, for a walk. Quite by accident, they had ended up at the Kingswood Shopping Mall.

"That was a disaster!" Alex remembered, clapping her hand to her forehead.

"At least this time we don't have T-Bone," giggled Lorraine.

"We may wish that we had T-Bone," Julie remarked. "We might need him to help carry all the cans that we are going to collect."

"Brussels sprouts, that's right," Alex groaned. "We need something to put all the cans in."

"How about paper sacks?" Janie suggested.

"My mom would really wonder what we were doing if we went back inside for paper sacks," Alex replied.

"Besides, who wants to lug around sacks full of cans?" Lorraine put in.

"I got it!" Alex snapped her fingers. "Let's use the wagon." She led the girls to the garage and opened the door.

Looking about, Alex spied the red wagon parked next to the wheelbarrow at the back of the garage. She was just about to pull it out of the garage when Mother suddenly opened the door that led from the kitchen to the garage.

"I thought I heard the garage door open!" Mother exclaimed when she saw Alex and the other girls. "What are you doing?"

"Uh, we thought we'd, uh, take turns riding in the wagon," Alex stuttered.

"Aren't you girls a little old for that?" Mother asked.

"Oh, yeah, maybe," Alex replied. "But it's fun anyway."

Mother shook her head and went back into the house. Alex pulled the wagon out of the garage and on up the driveway.

"Whew!" she exclaimed to her friends when she was safely out of hearing distance from the house. "How can mothers be so nosey?"

"That's what makes them mothers," Janie explained.

The girls laughed and skipped down the street. The wagon rolled noisily behind them. They were off on a new adventure and that was always exciting.

CHAPTER 4

Corn,
Beans,
Tomatoes,
and Soup!

As soon as the girls had gone far enough down Juniper Street to be out of sight of Alex's mother, they began to knock on neighbors' doors.

"Let's go to this house first," decided Julie. She and Alex led the way up the front walk. Janie and Lorraine hung back, suddenly shy.

"Hello, Mrs. Schmidt," Alex said politely as soon as the woman opened her door. "We are collecting cans of food for our church to give to poor people at Easter. Would you have any extra cans for us?"

"Well, Alex, that's a very nice thing for you girls to do," Mrs. Schmidt beamed back at Alex. "Wait right here!"

Mrs. Schmidt disappeared for a few moments. When she returned, she handed Alex a can of soup and a can of corn.

"Thank you very much, Mrs. Schmidt," Alex responded. She put the cans in the wagon.

At the next house, Alex repeated her speech. She was rewarded with three cans of stewed tomatoes.

"Ooooo-ick!" Janie turned up her nose after they had left the house.

"Now, Janie," Alex laughed. "It doesn't matter what is in the cans. They will all help to fill up the Easter basket."

The girls journeyed from house to house. Almost everyone gave them something to put in the wagon.

"Brussels sprouts, this wagon is getting heavy to pull," Alex soon complained. At the bottom of the hill, they had crossed to the other side of the street and now had to walk up the hill.

The wagon contained almost two full layers of cans.

"I'll pull it for awhile," Janie offered.

Alex held the wagon's handle out to Janie. Thinking that Janie had already grabbed the handle, Alex turned her back and began to walk to the front door of yet another house.

Janie, however, had not taken hold of the handle. She was bending down, busy tying her shoe. Before anyone could stop it, the wagon began to roll backwards down the street.

About the same time that the wagon began to roll, a car pulled around the corner at the bottom of Juniper Street and started up the hill. It looked very much like the wagon was going to smack right into the car!

"OH, NO!" all four girls screamed at once.

The car quickly swerved, barely missing the wagon by inches. The wagon continued its downward plunge until its wheels struck a pile of pebbles in the road, causing it to hit the curb and tip over. The cans spilled out of the wagon and began to roll down the street.

"BRUSSELS SPROUTS!" hollered Alex. She began to chase the cans. So did the other girls, doing their best to catch up with the cans of corn, beans, tomatoes, and soup!

"Hurry! Grab them before another car comes up the street and squishes them!" cried Janie. She hopped from can to can, grabbing first one and then another, awkwardly juggling them in her arms.

Lorraine had set the wagon right side up and was busily throwing can after can back inside it.

Alex stopped cans with her feet, soccer fashion. She called for Lorraine to bring the wagon to a pile she had collected.

"Oh, no!" Julie shouted suddenly. Alex turned to see her friend drop to her hands and knees at the side of the street.

"One of the cans just rolled down the drain to the sewer!" Julie announced.

"Well, stop them! Don't let them go down there!" Alex responded.

"I couldn't help it," Julie replied. "That one rolled too fast for me to catch."

Julie plopped herself down in front of the drain and caught all the rest of the cans that rolled in her direction.

Lorraine pulled the wagon around and helped load whatever cans each girl had collected. Finally, all the cans were safely back inside the wagon—all but the one that had slipped into the sewer.

"I hope it was a stewed tomatoes can," Janie commented as she peered down the drain opening with Alex. The drain was too dark. No one could see the can at its bottom.

"Oh, well, at least we only lost one of them," Alex replied. She quickly counted the cans. "Thirty-three!" she announced triumphantly.

"Wow! That ought to fill our Easter basket right up!" said Janie happily.

"Yeah, nobody will believe it when we bring thirty-three cans to Sunday school," said Alex.

"Uh, Alex," Janie suddenly frowned. "How are we going to get the cans to Sunday school if we don't tell our parents about them? I don't think I can hide thirty-three cans in my purse!"

Alex laughed. "Don't worry, Janie. I'm going to tell my parents about the cans. I just have to wait for the right time."

"Well, what are you going to do with the cans in the meantime?" Julie asked Alex. "Should we hide them somewhere?"

Alex looked puzzled. "I guess we better," she nodded.

"Where?" her friends wanted to know.

"Well, we could hide them in the bushes in the backyard," Alex suggested.

"Naw," Janie replied. "It could rain and get them all yucky. Besides, your parents might find them there."

"Yeah," Alex agreed.

"How about your tree house?" Lorraine offered.

"Great idea!" Alex responded. But then she frowned. "No, Rudy would find them there and tell Mom about them."

"I know the perfect place!" Julie suddenly announced. "You could hide them under your bed."

"Under my bed?" Alex asked, surprised at the suggestion.

"Sure!" Julie said. "We put some cans under our jackets, sneak them into the house, and stash 'em under your bed!"

"That is a perfect place!" agreed Alex.

"Until your mother decides to clean under the bed," Janie pointed out.

"Janie's right. It's too risky," Alex finally decided.

"Then where are we . . . ?" started Lorraine.

"I've got it!" Alex snapped her fingers. "This really is the perfect place. But we'll have to be extra sneaky."

"Where?" the others asked at once.

But Alex did not answer. Alarm quickly spread over her face. "Brussels sprouts!" she yelled. "Quick! Hide those cans! Rudy and Jason are coming down the street!"

The girls quickly ripped off their jackets and threw them over the cans in the wagon. Then Lorraine threw herself down on top of the jackets and the cans.

"What are you doing with the wagon?" Rudy asked Alex as soon as he and Jason reached the girls.

"What does it look like we're doing?" Alex replied in typical big-sister fashion. "We're giving each other rides in the wagon." Alex began pulling Lorraine and the wagon up the hill.

"Really?" said Rudy. "Can we have a turn?"

"No!" Alex snapped. "We just want to play by ourselves."

"Aren't you a little old to be giving each other rides in the wagon?" Jason wanted to know. "I didn't think you still did that in fifth grade."

Alex didn't answer. She rolled her eyes at the other girls.

"Aw, come on, Alex, give us a ride!" Rudy whined. He started to climb in the wagon with Lorraine.

"NO!" Alex shouted. "The wagon's already too heavy!"

Indeed, with Lorraine and thirty-three cans piled inside, the wagon was almost impossible to pull. Alex felt the sweat break out on her forehead as she strained to pull it up the hill.

"Alex, you shouldn't say that Lorraine is too fat to ride in the wagon," Rudy teased.

"I didn't say that, you little nerd," shot back Alex.

"You said the wagon was too heavy," Jason pointed out.

"So, that means that Lorraine's too heavy," laughed Rudy. He and Jason danced around the wagon laughing and pointing at Lorraine. Poor Lorraine! Her face turned bright red.

"GET OUT OF HERE!" Alex yelled at Rudy and Jason. She chased the two younger boys a ways down the hill.

Lorraine climbed out of the wagon but left the jackets on top of the cans to hide them. The girls quickly pulled the wagon the rest of the way up the hill.

"Let's hide these cans fast before Rudy and Jason come back," Janie suggested.

"Follow me." Alex grinned and led the way back to her house. As quietly as possible, Alex rolled the wagon across the grass to the driveway. Cautiously, she pushed open the garage door. Leading her friends inside the garage, she pointed up to the rafters. Several boards lay on top of the rafters, making a high platform.

"We can put the cans up there on top of those boards," Alex said proudly. "Nobody will ever find them up there!"

"But how do we get them up there?" Janie asked.

"Easy!" Alex replied. "Rudy and I have been up there a few times. We just pull the ladder over and climb up."

"I'll get the ladder!" Julie volunteered a little too loudly.

"Shh!" Alex warned. "My mom might hear you. She's right inside."

"Sorry," said Julie. She reached for the ladder and managed to unhook it from its place along a wall. But Julie did not get a proper grip on it, and the ladder swung backwards over her head. It crashed into the other side of the garage, knocking down Father's rakes, shovels, and garden clippers.

CRASH! BANG! CLATTER! The noise was deafening. The girls ducked and covered their heads. Things crashed all around them. The ladder slid to the floor an inch away from Julie.

Suddenly, the very thing happened that Alex had tried to avoid. The door to the kitchen opened. Mother appeared in the doorway.

"ALEX!" she called immediately. "WHAT IS GOING ON OUT THERE?"

CHAPTER 5

A Treasure Walk

"Uh, sorry about the noise, Mom." Alex straightened to a standing position. She pushed a broom away that had fallen against her shoulder. It fell to the floor with a bang.

"What happened?" Mother asked. She stood with her hands on her hips looking at the clutter on the garage floor.

"We were, uh, bringing in the wagon to, uh, put it away and we accidentally knocked over the ladder," Alex stammered.

"Is anybody hurt?" Mother asked in concern.

"No," the girls all assured her.

"Well, pick it up," said Mother and went back into the house.

"Whew!" Alex wiped her forehead and sank down onto the wagon. "That was a close call!"

Janie shook her head at her best friend. "Alex, don't you think you should tell your mother the truth?"

"Of course I should, Janie," Alex sighed, "but I just can't right now. Besides, I didn't really tell a lie. I just didn't tell her the whole truth. We are going to put the wagon away as soon as we empty out the cans."

The girls picked the ladder up off the floor and steadied it against the rafters. Carefully, Alex and Julie climbed the ladder. Alex went all the way to the top, and Julie halted her climb at the middle. Janie and Lorraine handed the cans of food to Julie, and Julie passed them on up to Alex.

They worked as fast as they could. Alex was afraid that Mother might open the door again at any moment. Finally, the last can was placed in its spot. Alex and Julie climbed down the ladder and quickly hung it back up on its hooks.

"Brussels sprouts! I'm glad that's done!" Alex exclaimed in relief.

"Not quite," Janie reminded her. "We still have to clean up the garage."

"Oh, yeah." Alex frowned at all the garden tools that still lay on the garage floor.

"Well, let's get at it," Lorraine said cheerfully as she picked up a rake. "You know, Alex, whenever I come over to your house, I can always count on one thing."

"Huh? What's that?" Alex asked.

"I know that we will not be bored," replied Lorraine with a grin. The girls all laughed and hurried to hang Father's tools back on the walls.

The next evening, Alex and Rudy joined their older sister, Barbara, on the front porch. Rudy and Alex hopped onto the porch swing while Barbara relaxed in a wicker chair. Mother soon arrived and sank into another chair. They were all waiting for Father.

It was Tuesday evening and that meant that it was time for another exciting Treasure Hunt. Every Tuesday, the family would get together to read or talk about a story from the Bible. They would see how that story fit into their own lives. Discovering God's messages for their lives was the treasure for which they hunted.

Tonight, Father had asked that the family meet on the front porch for their Treasure Hunt. As soon as Father appeared, Alex and Rudy frowned.

"You aren't wearing your sea captain's hat," Alex complained to her father. He usually wore the hat with the bright red plume to the family Treasure Hunts.

"That's because we are going to do something different tonight," Father replied. "We are going to take a walk together."

"Oh, good!" Alex and Rudy shouted at once. They started to run off the porch but Father stopped them.

"I need to give some directions first," he told them. "I want Barbara to go that way." He pointed down the street to the left. "And I want Alex to go that way." He pointed up the street in the opposite direction.

"But Dad . . . " Alex tried to interrupt.

"And I want Rudy to go across the street," Father continued, ignoring Alex.

"And Mother should go behind the house and through the backyards."

"But Dad," Rudy shouted, "we can't take a walk together like that!"

"We can't?" Father asked. "Why not?"

"Because we would all be going in different directions," Rudy explained.

Father pretended to look confused and scratched his head. "You know, I think you're right," he told Rudy. "I guess we all need to go in the same direction. Well, which way do you want to go?" he asked.

"That way," Rudy pointed down the hill.

"Okay," Father agreed. He and Rudy began to walk and the rest of the family followed.

"Well, this is fun," Father commented after they had walked a ways. "It's nice to take a walk together, isn't it? Besides walking in the same direction, what else do you do when you take a walk with a friend?"

"You laugh a lot," Alex replied. She and her older sister, Barbara, had been giggling ever since Father had tried to send them off in different directions.

Father nodded. "Yes, you laugh and talk and feel close to your friend, don't you? What if you were to take a walk with the same person every day? Would you get to know that person very well?"

"Oh, yeah," Alex replied. "You'd probably become best friends!"

"Very good, Firecracker," Father said. "You are right. You would become best friends. And when you are best friends with someone, you begin to act alike and talk alike and think alike, don't you?"

"Yes," they all agreed.

"Can you think of anything else that you do when you walk with a friend?" Father asked.

"Well, you usually decide where you're going," Barbara answered. "You might walk to a store or to school or just around the block."

Father nodded his head. "That's right. You and your friend have a common goal. You know where you are going."

"You also walk at the same pace," Mother added. "You can't go faster or slower than your friend or you won't stay together."

"Yes," Father agreed. "Now let's repeat what we have learned about taking a walk with a friend. You and your friend need to go in the same direction. You both talk and laugh and become close to one another. You have a common goal, and you both walk at the same pace.

"What would you say, if I were to tell you that you could have a very special walk with a very special friend and that friend is God? In fact," Father went on, "your whole life could be one long walk with God."

"Brussels sprouts!" Alex exclaimed. "If your whole life was a walk with God, would you become His best friend?"

"Absolutely," Father told her. "In fact, the Bible gives us the names of some of God's best friends who did just that very thing. They spent their lives walking with God."

"Who?" the children asked.

"Well, in the Book of Genesis, it says that Abraham, Isaac, and Noah walked with God. We all know what great things those men accomplished in their lives. But there's another person who is mentioned as having walked with God that you may not have heard about."

"Who's that?" Rudy asked.

"Enoch," Father replied.

"Enoch?" Alex frowned. "Who was that?"

"He's one of the early, early people in the Bible," Father replied. "He's the great, great, great, great grandson of Adam. And Enoch is rather special. In Hebrews, the Bible tells us that Enoch never died! God took Enoch up to heaven so that Enoch would not suffer death. It says that before God took him, Enoch was told that he was pleasing to God."

"Wow!" Rudy whistled. "Enoch must have been God's very best friend!"

Father laughed. "Enoch was very, very close to God," he said. "We can also be very, very close to God. We can walk with Him, too. The same things apply when we walk with God as when we walk with other friends. We need to find out the direction our lives should take. We need to talk to Him and laugh with Him. We need to ask Him what goals to set for our lives, and we need to keep pace with Him."

"But how do you tell what direction God wants you to go?" Rudy looked puzzled.

"That's a good question," Father replied. "You need to ask God that question in prayer. But you can also get a lot of answers by reading the Bible. Think of the Bible as a traffic signal. It tells you when to go and when to stop and when to turn. It would let you know if you were about to go in the wrong direction."

"Do you mean that if you were about to go in the wrong direction, the Bible would stop you from doing it?" Rudy asked his father.

"Yes," Father answered.

"How?" Rudy wanted to know.

"Well," Father's eye twinkled, "let's talk about how following the Bible could have stopped you and Alex from throwing that grapefruit in the store last week."

"Oh, no!" Alex and Rudy shuddered. They didn't want to remember the trouble they had caused at the grocery store.

"There are several Bible verses that should have stopped you from throwing that grapefruit. One of them is "Do unto others as you would have them do unto you."

"Do you mean that because we

wouldn't want someone else throwing around our grapefruit, we shouldn't throw around the store's grapefruit?" Alex asked.

"Very well put, Firecracker," replied Father.

"But we don't have any grapefruit," Rudy said, frowning at them.

Father rubbed his chin in a thoughtful way. "No, but let's say that you and Alex decide to set up a lemonade stand. You have a supply of real lemons that you use to make your lemonade. Now, what if a couple of your friends came along and started throwing around your lemons and ended up spilling all the lemons onto the street? Wouldn't you be upset about that?"

"Yes," Rudy admitted.

"Well, that's how the store manager felt about your throwing around his grapefruit and spilling his apples," Father explained. "And, according to the Bible, you should only do things to people that you would want done to you. So if you had been following the Bible and walking with God, you would not have thrown that grapefruit."

"Yeah, I get it," said Rudy. "You only want good things to happen to you, so you should only do good things to others."

"Exactly!" replied Father.

"You know what?" Rudy asked his father.

"What?" Father answered.

"Tonight, we shouldn't call this a Treasure Hunt. We should call it a Treasure Walk!"

The family laughed. They continued their walk down the street, laughing and talking merrily—all except Alex. She had suddenly experienced an uneasy feeling in the pit of her stomach.

What about all those cans of food she had hidden in the garage? She had certainly not walked with God when she had sneaked them up to the rafters.

And, what about not telling her

mother the whole truth? That had not been walking with God, either.

"Brussels sprouts," Alex said to herself. "I almost wish I hadn't done those things."

CHAPTER 6

Parking Lot Sneak

All that week and the next, Alex tried to think of a way to get the hidden cans of food to Sunday school. Somehow, she would have to sneak the cans into the church without anyone else in her family knowing about it. But how could she do that? Finally, one Sunday morning, Alex carried out a desperate plan.

Early that morning, Alex sneaked downstairs very quietly. To avoid making any noise, she carried her shoes in her hands. She did not want to risk waking up the rest of the family.

Once downstairs, Alex slipped on her shoes and grabbed a sack out of the kitchen closet. She hurried to the door that led to the garage. She opened the door very quietly and raced down the steps into the garage.

Alex planned to collect a few cans from their hiding place in the rafters, stuff them in a sack, and hide them under the front seat of the car. Then, after her family drove to church, she would sneak the cans out of the car and take them into Sunday school.

It seemed like a wonderful plan; however, she had forgotten one thing. Her father always parked the car in the garage at night, and there it was—right underneath the very rafters that she needed to reach. What should she do now? She couldn't possibly get the ladder up to the rafters with the car in the way.

After hesitating for a few moments, Alex kicked off her shoes and pulled herself onto the car's hood. She then cautiously climbed up on top of its roof. It was perfect—even better than the ladder! She could easily reach the cans.

Opening the sack, Alex dropped six cans of food into it. She did not think any more cans would fit under the car seat. Closing the sack, Alex slid down the windshield to the hood and off the hood to the floor.

As quietly as possible, Alex opened the back door to the family station wagon and crammed the sack under the front seat. She made sure that no one could see it. Then she closed the door and ran back into the house.

Carefully, Alex locked the door to the garage and scurried through the house and back up the stairs to her bedroom. Leaping into bed, Alex pulled the covers up to her chin and shivered with excitement at what she had done.

She could hardly wait to bring the cans to her Sunday school class and put them in the girls' Easter basket. She giggled as she imagined the look on Janie's face when she plopped six cans

into the basket. Why, if all the other girls brought a can or two, they would surely be way ahead of the boys!

Alex lay awake until it was time for the rest of her family to get up. She dressed quickly and beat everyone down to the breakfast table. She made sure that she was the first one to the car and took her place in the back seat on the same side as the sack full of cans. She did not want Barbara or Rudy to accidentally discover the sack.

Unfortunately, Alex's plans were ruined when her sister, Barbara, dashed out to the car at the last minute and flung open the car door on Alex's side.

"Move over!" Barbara demanded, trying to force her way into Alex's spot.

"No!" Alex refused to budge. "I was here first."

"Alex! I want to get in," Barbara told her with a frown.

"Well, get in on the other side," Alex retorted.

"I don't want to walk around to the other side." Barbara's voice rose to a shout. "Let me in here!"

"No! This is my spot!" Alex yelled back.

"Alex," Father entered the conversation, "let your sister into the car. We are going to be late for church."

"But, Dad—" Alex began.

"ALEX!" Father said in his most commanding voice.

Alex moved over to the middle of the back seat. She made a point of not looking at or speaking to anyone else in the car the entire way to church. She did, however, keep an eye on Barbara's feet, hoping that her sister would not stretch her feet under the seat and kick the sack full of cans.

The ride to church seemed to take forever. By the time they got there, Alex was a nervous wreck. She quickly slid out of the car on Rudy's side. Hoping that her father would not notice, Alex left the door unlocked on that side.

Walking briskly, Alex entered the church building ahead of her family and turned down the hall to her Sunday school class. She did not go into the classroom. Instead, she waited in the hallway until Janie arrived.

"Hi, Alex!" Janie loudly greeted her friend.

"Shhhhh! Come on!" Alex grabbed Janie's arm and pulled her around a corner, down another hallway, and out a side door of the church.

"What's going on?" Janie demanded, jerking her arm away from Alex.

Alex did not answer but peered around the corner of the building into the parking lot. It was almost empty. Just a few latecomers were hurrying to the front door.

"What's going on?" Janie repeated, coming to stand beside Alex.

"I have to get something out of my car, but I don't want anyone to see me," Alex explained.

"Why not?" Janie looked puzzled.

"Because if my parents found out, I would get clobbered!" replied Alex.

Janie rolled her eyes at Alex. "Does this have anything to do with the cans of food hidden in your garage?"

"Yes," Alex admitted. She told Janie how she had sneaked downstairs that morning, had grabbed six cans from the rafters, and had hidden the cans under the front seat of the family station wagon.

"Alex!" Janie exclaimed shaking her head. "What happens when your parents find out about all of this? They always do find out, you know."

"I know, I know," Alex answered. "But right now, I don't want to think about it. I just want to win the Easter basket contest."

"Okay," Janie sighed. "What do you want me to do?"

"Be a lookout for me," Alex told her. "Let me know if you see anyone coming—you know, whistle or something."

Before Janie could reply, Alex took off running. She kept close to the building, trying her best to keep out of sight behind trees and bushes, as she made her way to the parking lot where the family station wagon was parked.

As usual, her father had parked the car right in front of a wall of windows that made up the southern part of the church sanctuary. At this moment, her parents were in the sanctuary attending the worship service. What if they happened to look out a window and see Alex sneaking into the car? Alex tried not to think about it.

Pushing this thought from her mind, Alex darted behind a row of cars, keeping low to the ground. She dashed from one car to another until she was directly behind her own car.

Glancing behind her, Alex saw Janie raise her hand in the air with her thumb pointing to the sky. It was the all clear sign. Alex gulped. It was now or never!

With her heart thumping wildly, Alex crawled to one side of the station wagon—the side she had left unlocked. She hoped that her father had not checked the locks before going into church. Very cautiously, Alex reached for the door. Click-clack! It opened. Alex breathed a sigh of relief.

Just as she was about to open the door wide enough to crawl into the car, a loud crash sounded directly in front of her.

The front doors of the church slammed open and a herd of kindergartners rushed outside, followed by a harassed Sunday school teacher!

Just in time, Alex dove headfirst into the car and pulled the car door shut behind her. Lying flat on the back seat, Alex hoped that the teacher had not seen her.

The children's noises soon faded into the distance. Peeking out a window, Alex saw that the kindergartners had gone to the playground located on the other side of the parking lot.

Alex looked for Janie. She was nowhere in sight. She must have gone back around the building to get away from the kindergartners, Alex guessed.

Reaching under the front seat, Alex yanked out the sack full of cans. Forcing herself to act calmly, she slipped out of the car, barely latching the door to avoid any loud noises, and darted from car to car back the way she had come.

Just as she had thought, Alex found Janie waiting for her at the back of the building. With sighs of relief, the two girls hurried inside.

"I don't know how you do it, Alex. I don't know how you get me into all these crazy things." Janie shook her head as she and Alex headed for their Sunday school room.

"I just want to keep your life interesting, Janie," Alex told her best friend with a grin.

"Ha, ha, ha! Very funny!" Janie replied as they walked through the doorway and into the fifth grade classroom.

"Sorry, we're late," Alex apologized to Mrs. Winthrop.

"That's all right." Mrs. Winthrop smiled at Alex and Janie. "We were just adding some cans of food to the Easter baskets."

"I brought some, too," Alex told her teacher. She dumped her six cans into the girls' Easter basket. She smiled to see several other cans lying in the basket. It was filling up nicely. But when Alex compared the girls' basket to the boys' basket, her mouth dropped open in horror. The boys' basket had more in it. Furthermore, someone had stuck a giant canned ham in the middle of the basket!

"Brussels sprouts! Who put this ham in here?" Alex cried out loud.

"I did," replied Joshua Barton. "What's it to you?"

"Yeah," the other boys joined in. "You better watch out. The boys are going to win the contest!"

"They are not," Alex retorted. "The girls are going to win!" She tossed her head and stomped to the front of the room to take a seat beside Janie. She tried to act as if it didn't matter, but secretly, she was worried. The boys were ahead of the girls and there were only three more weeks until Palm Sunday!

CHAPTER 7

Tuna and T-Bone

After school one day, Alex sprawled with Rudy and Jason on Jason's front lawn. It was an unusually warm spring day, and Jason had brought Miss Muff and the kittens out to enjoy the fresh air and sunshine.

The kittens were just beginning to explore outside their box and would pounce and fall on one another, looking like tangled little balls of fluff and feet.

Miss Muff watched her kittens tumble on the grass and occasionally gave one a lick or a bat with her paw. She looked very proud and purred constantly.

"I think Miss Muff makes a good

mother, don't you?" Jason asked.

Alex and Rudy agreed.

"She's going to be so sad when we have to give her kittens away," Jason sighed wistfully.

"Maybe we can keep one, and then Miss Muff can see it every day," Alex suggested.

"Oh, that would be great!" Jason brightened. "Which one do you want?"

"This one," Alex held up one of the kittens. It was a little female with soft, silky, gray hair.

"What made you pick that kitten?" Jason asked Alex.

"I didn't pick her," Alex admitted. "She picked me."

"Huh?" both boys looked puzzled.

"Well, it happened like this," Alex started to explain. "Whenever I visited the kittens, this little, gray kitten was always the first to come over to me. No matter how many people were around, she would always pick me. My dad says that sometimes animals will pick out their owners. T-Bone was like that. When my dad went to pick out a dog, T-Bone ran up to him and bit his finger the very first time he saw him. Dad said he knew right away that T-Bone was the dog for him!"

Jason and Rudy laughed. "Well, if this kitten has picked you, then you'd better keep her," said Jason.

"I'm trying my best to talk Mom into it," Alex sighed. "She just won't tell me yes or no."

"What about your dad?" asked Jason.

"Oh, he loves animals," Alex replied. "He'd have a whole zoo of them in the house if Mom would let him."

The boys laughed again.

"Do you think I could take this kitten inside our house?" Alex asked Jason. "Maybe if Mom saw how cute she's getting, she'd let me keep her."

"Oh, sure. Take her for as long as you like," Jason offered.

Grabbing up the little, gray kitten, Alex scurried into the house. She found Mother in the kitchen. She was dipping pieces of chicken into a large bowl of flour and then placing the flour-coated pieces into a shallow baking pan.

"Hi, Mom," Alex greeted her mother. "I've brought you a little visitor."

"Oh, how nice." Mother smiled at Alex and the kitten and went on dipping her chicken.

"I have thought of a name for this kitten if you let me keep her," Alex told her mother. "I would call her Tuna."

"Tuna?" Mother rolled her eyes.

"Don't you think that's a great name for a cat?" Alex asked. "I'm sure any cat would like that name. Besides," she added, "it goes well with T-Bone, don't you think?"

"Hmmmph!" Mother snorted. "Don't get your hopes up too high. I haven't said that you can keep the kitten."

"I know, I know," Alex said. "But look

and see how cute she is." Alex placed the
kitten on the counter beside Mother's
flour bowl.

"Alex! Get that cat off the kitchen
counter!" Mother ordered.

"Aw, Mom, you scared her," Alex
complained, picking up the kitten and
snuggling it in her arms. "She's just a
baby, you know."

"I don't care," Mother replied firmly.
"No animal is allowed on my kitchen
counter."

Just then, the family dog poked his head around the door to the kitchen. His afternoon nap had been disturbed by the loud voices in the kitchen.

"Hi, T-Bone," Alex called to the black Labrador. "Come here and see Tuna."

"Woof!" T-Bone wagged his tail happily and bounded into the room. The kitchen was his favorite room in the house, especially when it was filled with the aroma of something good to eat. T-Bone walked over to where Mother was working on the chicken and sniffed the air hungrily.

"T-Bone, I'd like you to meet Tuna." Alex held the kitten under the big dog's nose. T-Bone took a big sniff.

That was too much for the kitten. "YEOW! MEOW! HISS!" she screeched. Flinging herself backward out of Alex's arms and onto the kitchen counter, the kitten crashed into Mother's flour bowl, sending it and a piece of chicken flying onto the floor!

"AHHHHH!" cried Mother. She just barely caught the pan of chicken before it, too, sailed to the floor.

"Brussels sprouts!" Alex cried in alarm. She dived for the kitten, catching her in the air a moment before she, too, crashed to the floor.

"Gotcha!" Alex exclaimed. She turned to look at her mother who was on the floor wrestling with T-Bone. White flour covered everything, including Mother and the dog.

"Give me that chicken, T-Bone!" Mother demanded loudly, prying the big dog's mouth open. T-Bone had caught the piece of floured chicken when it had been knocked off the counter.

The dog did not want to give up his prize piece of chicken. He gripped it in his teeth and would not let go as Mother pulled on another part of the chicken. Finally, after Mother strongly insisted several times, T-Bone let her have the chicken.

"Good dog," Mother sighed and patted T-Bone's head. She frowned as she looked at the mangled piece of chicken.

"Uh, sorry, Mom," Alex meekly apologized. "I guess I should take Tuna outside now, huh?"

"Right, Alex," Mother replied. "Then come back in here and help me clean up this mess."

"Okay," called Alex as she ran out the front door. "Oh, why did you have to do that?" she asked the frightened kitten as soon as they were outside. "You might have just spoiled any chance I had of keeping you."

"Mew," the kitten answered and ducked her head under Alex's arm.

The next week at school, Alex and Janie sat at the lunch table with Julie and Lorraine and moaned about the Easter baskets at Sunday school.

"You should have seen it," Alex sighed. "When we got there, the boys had added eleven cans to their basket! That was a lot more than the girls added. I wish I could bring more than six cans at a time."

"Did you sneak more cans to church?" Julie asked, surprised.

"Yes," Alex admitted, "but I can only take six of them at a time. That's all that will fit under the seat."

"That means that you've brought twelve cans to Sunday school so far," counted Julie. "That's pretty good."

"Not good enough," answered Alex gloomily. "The boys are really determined to beat us and have brought more cans than the girls. Then, of course, there's Joshua Barton's canned ham that practically fills the basket itself."

"So why don't you bring a ham?" suggested Julie.

"Where am I going to get a canned ham?" Alex wanted to know. "I'm having enough trouble collecting green beans!"

When Alex got home from school one

day the following week, she found what she thought was an answer to Joshua's ham. Mother had asked her to get a package of frozen fish from the freezer in the basement. In searching through the freezer for the fish, Alex had uncovered a big frozen turkey. It was then that the idea came to her.

"A turkey!" Alex whispered to herself. Wouldn't that be the perfect addition to the girls' Easter basket! It would fill up the basket even more than a canned ham.

Grinning to herself, Alex hurried upstairs to call Janie. She wanted to see what her best friend thought about her idea.

"Alex, are you crazy!" Janie exclaimed. "You really want to take your mother's frozen turkey to Sunday school?"

"Sure," Alex replied. "The turkey is a lot bigger than Joshua's ham."

"But Alex, don't you think your mother might miss the turkey?" asked Janie.

"Well, maybe," Alex admitted. "But there are so many other things in the freezer, that maybe she might forget about it."

"I dunno, Alex. I don't think you better do it."

"Aw, come on, Janie," Alex pleaded. "We can't let the boys win the Easter basket contest. If they win, Joshua Barton will never let us forget it!"

"Well, since you put it that way. . . . " Janie gave in. "What can I do to help?"

"Tell me what you think I ought to do," said Alex. "Right now, the turkey is too big to fit under the car seat, but what if I thawed it out? Do you think then I could squish it down to make it fit?"

"I dunno," Janie replied. "Why are you asking me?"

"Because you are the only one I have to ask!" retorted Alex loudly.

"Okay, okay, take it easy," Janie said quickly. "I guess you should thaw it out if you want to fit it under the car seat.

And you probably ought to take it out of the freezer right away, because my mom says it takes a long time for turkeys to thaw."

"Really?" Alex frowned. "Does it take more than six days? That's how many days there are until Palm Sunday."

"Maybe," Janie replied. "It might even take longer."

"Brussels sprouts," Alex said. "I better get it outta there fast. But where am I going to hide it until Sunday?"

"Why not hide it in your closet?" Janie suggested.

"Good idea, Janie! You're a genius!" Alex replied and hung up the phone.

That evening, while her parents were busy in the kitchen, Alex hurried down the basement steps to the freezer. She carried a large, plastic trash bag. Heaving the turkey out of the freezer, Alex slid it into the trash sack. It was heavy!

Slowly, Alex lugged the huge turkey to the stairway and climbed back up the basement stairs. Huffing and puffing, she had almost reached the top step when Rudy and Jason suddenly appeared around the corner and began to clatter down the steps very quickly.

"Look out!" Alex cried as they jostled her and the bag of turkey. She strained to keep her balance and might have succeeded except that, at that moment, T-Bone whipped around the corner and ran straight into her.

"AHHHHHHH!" Alex cried as she tripped over the dog. She and the turkey bounced step by step down the stairs!

CHAPTER 8

Frozen Turkey Escape

"Are you all right, Alex?" Rudy asked. Alex sprawled at the foot of the basement steps. The sack with the turkey inside lay several feet away where it had slid after its fall from the top step.

"Ohhhhh . . ." Alex moaned.

"Alex, are you all right?" Rudy repeated.

"I guess so," answered Alex. She slowly stood up and rubbed her back. She looked back up the steps at her dog. T-Bone lay on the top step, his head down between his paws. His eyes begged Alex to forgive him for somehow causing another disaster.

"You mutt!" Alex scowled. She picked up the sack and climbed back up the stairs. Rudy and Jason went on to play. T-Bone thumped his tail hopefully on the top step as Alex reached him.

"Okay, I forgive you," Alex told the dog. "Now come on with me. We've got to get this turkey upstairs to my room."

Without further trouble, Alex made it through the rest of the house and up another set of stairs to her bedroom. Flinging open her closet door, Alex slid the sack and the turkey to the back of the closet. She then collapsed on her bed. T-Bone curled up beside her.

"Well, we got the turkey up here," Alex whispered in the dog's ear. "I just hope we can get it out to the car Sunday morning without any trouble."

"WOOF!" T-Bone agreed and laid his head to rest on Alex's stomach.

On the Saturday night before Palm Sunday, Janie stayed with Alex. The girls had decided to sneak the turkey out to the car that evening instead of waiting until morning. Janie was going to help Alex accomplish the task.

"It's a good thing we're doing this tonight," Alex told Janie. "My closet is beginning to smell like a turkey. I have been so afraid Mom would notice it. It's also been hard keeping T-Bone out of the closet!"

"I bet," Janie giggled. "T-Bone probably thinks your closet smells wonderful."

The girls waited until Mother had finished cleaning up after dinner and had left the kitchen. Then very carefully and very quietly, they made their way down the stairs and through the house to the back door.

Opening the back door quietly, the two girls sneaked outside with their bundle. It was very dark, but Alex did not dare turn on the outside light. Circling around the house, the girls approached the driveway where the family car was parked.

"Let's hurry up and get this turkey into the car," Janie exclaimed. "This is kind of scary!"

The girls hurried to the car. They were just about to open the back door when, all of a sudden, Father popped up from the front seat.

"AHHHHHHHHH!" both girls screamed. They quickly dropped the turkey under the back end of the car.

"Dad!" Alex finally managed to say. "What are you doing out here?"

"Hello, girls," Father replied. He crawled out of the car and switched off a flashlight. "I was looking for an earring that your mother has lost. She thought it might have fallen off in the car."

"Oh," Alex said. "Did you, uh, find it?"

"No," answered Father, "but I'm ready to go back inside. Come on, girls. It's getting chilly out here."

There was nothing else for the girls to do but to follow Alex's father into the house. Once inside, Alex got Janie alone and said, "We gotta go back out there and get that turkey off of the driveway and into the car."

But that was not so easily done. Every time Alex and Janie started for the back door, Mother or Father would begin to talk to them. They would then have to stay in the living room. It was almost as if Alex's parents guessed that the girls were up to something.

"I wonder where that dog is?" Mother finally remarked, looking at her watch. "I let him outside almost twenty minutes ago."

"You mean T-Bone is outside?" Alex exclaimed. She looked at Janie in alarm. Was twenty minutes enough time for a dog to eat a turkey?

"I let T-Bone outside about this time every night." Mother frowned at Alex. "Is there something wrong with that?"

"Oh, no," Alex replied, jumping up from her seat. "I'll go call him."

She ran to the front door. Janie followed her. The girls stepped out on the front porch and called T-Bone's name loudly.

"T-BONE! COME HERE, BOY!" Alex shouted.

"I think I see him," Janie nudged Alex and pointed at the driveway. There, barely visible in the shadows, was the outline of a large dog. He stood by the car, his nose to the ground.

"T-Bone!" Alex cried. She jumped off of the porch and began to run towards the dog.

"GRRRRRR!" T-Bone growled as Alex got near him.

"It's just me, T-Bone," Alex said. "Stop growling!"

"GRRRRRR!" the dog continued to growl. He picked something up in his teeth and trotted to the other side of the car.

"Oh no, T-Bone, is that the turkey?" cried Alex. She followed the dog around the car for a closer look. The plastic trash sack had been torn to pieces and so had the plastic wrapper that had covered the turkey. With powerful teeth, T-Bone had snatched up the turkey in his mouth.

"Brussels sprouts!" Alex wailed. She took a step nearer the dog.

T-Bone and his prize moved away.

"T-Bone, come back here!" Alex began to chase the big dog around the yard, the turkey hanging from his mouth and dragging on the ground.

"Alex! What is going on out here?" Mother stepped outside onto the porch. "T-Bone! What in the world do you have in your mouth?"

Mother stepped off the porch into the yard. She peered closer at the dog. "Ooooooh!" she suddenly cried. "He's got some kind of animal!"

"Don't worry, Mom," sighed Alex. "It's not alive."

"Of course it's not alive, Alex," replied Mother. "I can see that. What is it?"

"It's a turkey," Alex said limply. She sank to the ground and held her head in her hands.

"A turkey?" Mother repeated, puzzled. "Where would he get a turkey?"

"From your freezer," Alex answered, not daring to look at her mother.

"What are you talking about?" Mother demanded as she looked from Alex to Janie and back to Alex again.

Alex took a deep breath and said all in a rush, "I took the turkey from the freezer to put it in the car so we could take it to Sunday school and put it in the girls' Easter basket but T-Bone got hold of it first."

After Alex finished speaking, there was complete silence. Mother did not say a word but continued to stare at Alex for what seemed like a long, long time. The only sound that could be heard was T-Bone prancing about the yard, the turkey dangling from his mouth.

Finally, Mother spoke, "I can't believe it." She shook her head. "You girls had better come inside and tell me the whole story. I'm sure your father will want to hear it too."

"But what about T-Bone? We can't just leave him out here, can we?" Alex reminded her mother.

"No, we'd better catch him," Mother said slowly. "I don't suppose it's proper

to let your dog run around the neighborhood carrying a turkey. I had better call
your father to help."

But, as things would have it, before
Mother could call Father, a tremendous
crash occurred in the garage. As fast as
they could, Alex, Janie, and Mother
rushed through the house and into the
garage. There, half sitting and half lying
on the garage floor was Father. He was
surrounded by an assortment of cans of
vegetables. The ladder lay beside Father
as if it had been knocked to the ground.

"Can anyone tell me," Father roared,
looking straight at Alex, "why our garage
rafters were full of vegetables?"

CHAPTER 9

God's Race

Alex took a deep breath. She was really in for it now. Outside, the dog was running around with Mother's turkey clenched in his teeth. And here, in the garage, her father sat buried beneath a mound of cans that she had hidden in the rafters! Why, oh why, did the two catastrophes have to happen at the same time?

"Alex, something tells me that you know where all these cans of food came from," said Mother, tapping her foot.

"Uh, yeah," Alex admitted, looking down at the floor.

"Would you like to share that information with your parents?" Father

106

asked. He pushed two cans of green beans, one of corn, and two of stewed tomatoes off his lap. Slowly, he stood up and rubbed his legs.

"Well, we, uh, collected the cans from the neighbors," Alex began in a low voice.

"The neighbors!" Mother exclaimed. "You mean you asked our neighbors to give you cans of food?"

"Yes, for our Easter basket at Sunday school," Alex replied. "Oh, don't worry," she hastily added at the sight of her parents' faces. "We told them what we were going to do with the cans."

"But why in the world did you put the cans up in the rafters of our garage?" Father demanded.

"Because we were afraid you might make us take the cans back to the neighbors," Alex admitted.

"Humph!" Father snorted. He stood with his hands on his hips and stared at Alex. So did Mother.

"You should have asked our permission to collect cans from the neighbors," Father finally spoke. "I am very surprised and disappointed in you, Firecracker."

"I'm sorry." Alex hung her head. "I just wanted to win the Easter basket competition."

Father opened his mouth to reply but, at that moment, there was a loud pounding on the garage door. BAM! BAM! BAM!

Rushing to the door, Father raised it as fast as he could. There, on the other side of the door, stood a policeman.

"Hello, officer. What can I do for you?" asked Father in a surprised voice.

"Is this the Brackenbury residence?" the officer asked.

"Why, yes, it is," answered Father. "I'm Jim Brackenbury."

"Well, Mr. Brackenbury," said the policeman, "we have had a complaint from one of your neighbors."

"A complaint?" Father frowned. "What kind of a complaint?"

"A complaint about your dog," the policeman replied.

"Uh oh!" Alex, Janie, and Mother cried together.

"It seems that your dog has taken off with one of your neighbor's cats," the policeman continued.

"What!" Father exclaimed. "T-Bone would never do that!"

"Your neighbor across the street, Mrs. Goodrich, called us to report that her cat was missing. She said a large black dog, very much resembling your dog, had been seen running around the neighborhood with a rather large animal in its mouth. As Mrs. Goodrich has a rather large cat, she was afraid that it was her cat in your dog's mouth."

The policeman paused. Father looked stunned. Suddenly, Mother began to laugh. She laughed and laughed as if she could not stop. Father and the policeman looked at Mother as if she were out of her mind.

"I'm sorry," Mother gasped. "You see, T-Bone does not have a cat in his mouth. It's a turkey!"

"A turkey?" Father and the policeman asked together.

"I'm sure there is a further explanation to all of this," Father said in a hopeful voice.

"Oh, I'm sure there must be," Mother agreed and turned to motion Alex and Janie forward. "I believe the girls have the answer."

Right there, in front of the policeman, Alex and Janie had to explain how Alex had pulled the turkey out of the freezer and how she and Janie had carried it to the car, but had dropped it in the driveway after being startled by Father.

After hearing the story, neither Father nor the policeman could keep a straight face. They laughed especially hard when Alex told them how she had chased T-Bone around the yard, the turkey dangling from his mouth.

"Officer," Father said, putting his arms around the girls, "what kind of jail sentence do you give turkey snatchers?"

Alex and Janie gasped.

"I don't know," the officer admitted. "I've never caught any before."

"Hmmmm . . ." Father rubbed his chin. "I guess we'd better go catch that dog before other neighbors call the police."

After calling Barbara and Rudy to help in the chase, the Brackenbury family and Janie hunted for T-Bone and the turkey. They found him at the bottom of the Juniper Street hill. After several long chases, they managed to get T-Bone (carrying what was left of the turkey in his mouth) up the hill and into the backyard where they clanged shut the gate. Now, T-Bone and the turkey were safely caught behind the fence.

"Whew!" Father wiped his forehead. "I'm glad that's over."

"Not quite," Mother reminded him, looking at Alex and Janie.

"Oh, yes, girls, I believe we need to have a little talk," said Father.

Alex and Janie followed Father and Mother into the living room. In answering her parents' questions, Alex (with the help of Janie) told the whole story about how she and her friends had collected the cans of vegetables from the neighbors and hidden them in the rafters above the garage.

"I guess I wanted to win the contest so badly that I didn't think about all the wrong things I was doing," Alex told her parents. "I should have asked you if we could collect the cans. And I shouldn't have taken the turkey."

"You are right, Firecracker," said Father. "What you did was wrong. You said you did those things so that you could win, but you can't ever be a real winner if you have to sneak around and do bad things to win.

"You see," Father went on in a softer voice, "there are two kinds of winners. There are God's winners and there are the world's winners. The world's winners use any kind of method to win. They cheat, lie, and hurt other people to get ahead. But God's winners play by God's game rules which include honesty, fair play, and regard for others. And, in the end, God's winners come out way ahead of the world's winners. God's winners are the real winners.

"The Book of Hebrews tells us to run with patience the particular race that God has set before us. It says to put aside the things that would slow us down and keep us from winning God's race. One of the things that keeps us from winning God's race is dishonesty.

"You were dishonest, Firecracker, by not telling your mother and me about collecting the cans of vegetables and by hiding them in the garage. You were also dishonest by stealing the turkey out of the freezer. By doing those things, you actually made it impossible to win God's race. It was kind of like running the race with your legs tied together," Father chuckled.

"Brussels sprouts!" exclaimed Alex. "I guess I was pretty stupid. I wonder if I'll ever win God's race."

"Of course you will." Father put his arm around her. "But before you can run to win the race, you need to learn to walk with God every day."

"Oh, yeah," Alex replied. "I guess walking comes before running. It's like what you were talking about in our Treasure Hunt. By walking with God, I can become best friends with Him."

"Yes," Father said with a nod, "and you need to pay attention to His traffic signals. Now where do you find His traffic signals?"

"In the Bible," Alex answered.

"Right," said Father. "Read the Bible every day and you will get in good shape for God's race."

CHAPTER 10

An Easter Surprise

The next morning dawned clear and bright. It was Palm Sunday. Janie and Alex awoke early, the sunlight streaming through Alex's window with the promise of warm weather approaching.

"We're going to start softball practice in two weeks," Alex told Janie, sleepily.

"What did you say?" Janie stretched and rubbed the sleep out of her eyes.

"I said that softball practice starts in two weeks," yawned Alex. She sat up in bed and looked out of the window.

"So?" Janie frowned.

"So, I'm ready for summer and ball games," said Alex. She was the number one pitcher for her softball team, the Tornadoes.

Janie sat up and joined Alex at the window. "It almost looks like summer is here," she observed.

"Almost," Alex agreed, "except that we need more leaves on the trees."

The girls enjoyed the peaceful view from Alex's window until Mother's soft knock was heard at the door.

"Time to start getting ready for church," Mother announced. Alex and Janie looked at one another. Each remembered Alex's father saying that he did not think that Alex should benefit from her wrongdoing. She could not add any more cans of vegetables to the girls' Easter basket.

Instead, Father had suggested that Alex put the cans into the general food barrel at their church. That would mean that unless the other girls in the Sunday school class brought a lot of cans to church that morning, the boys would win the Easter basket contest. Alex and Janie could hardly stand to think of such a thing.

"We'll never hear the end of it from Joshua Barton," said Alex gloomily.

"No kidding," Janie agreed.

The girls dragged themselves out of bed. Janie went home to get ready for church. Alex got dressed and went downstairs.

On the way to church, Alex tried to think of what to say to Joshua Barton. He would be absolutely impossible when he learned that the boys had won the Easter basket contest. She finally decided that she would ignore him and act as if she didn't care.

When they arrived at church, Father and Alex carried in the last of the cans of vegetables that had fallen from the rafters the night before. Alex swallowed hard as she watched them slide down into the bottom of the large food barrel. If only she had been honest and had asked her parents if she could collect the cans, they might be safely nestled in the soft grass of the girls' Easter basket right now.

Father patted Alex's shoulder. "Time to go to Sunday school," he told her gently.

Alex shrugged and tried to saunter down the hallway as if she hadn't a care in the world. She found Janie waiting for her outside their classroom door.

"Alex! Guess what?" Janie cried excitedly. "The other girls have all brought cans—lots of them. We might win yet!"

"Really?" Alex raised her head in hope. She dashed into the classroom to look at the Easter baskets. It was impossible to tell which one was packed the fullest. Cans spilled from both as they overflowed with food.

"We will count the cans together," Mrs. Winthrop told her class as soon as everyone was seated at the big round table in the center of the room. "First,

let's count the cans in the girls' basket,"
she said.

"YEAH!" the girls all cried.

Mrs. Winthrop lugged the heavy
basket with pink ribbons to the table
and awkwardly set it down.

"I'll count them," Joshua Barton
offered. He leaned forward to grab at the
basket.

"Forget it!" Alex slammed her fist
down on top of Joshua's hand.

"I'll do the counting," Mrs. Winthrop

declared. She began pulling cans out of the basket. "One—two—three . . . " Mrs. Winthrop counted each can and stacked them all up in front of her.

"Whew! That's a lot of cans," she exclaimed when she was finished. There were thirty-eight cans of food in the girls' Easter basket.

Alex and Janie looked at one another hopefully. Maybe, just maybe, even with the canned ham, the girls might beat the boys!

Mrs. Winthrop then pulled the boys' Easter basket up to the table. "One— two—three . . . " she began to count its cans.

At the end of the count, Alex and Janie held their breath. "Thirty-five— thirty-six—thirty-seven . . . " Mrs. Winthrop felt around in the grass at the bottom of the basket. "Thirty-eight and thirty-nine," she said as she fished out two more cans from under the grass. "Looks to me like the boys have won with a total of thirty-nine cans."

Alex and Janie groaned. They'd come so close. To be beaten by only one can was almost more than they could bear.

"If only I would have had my parents permission to collect the cans from the neighbors," Alex moaned to Janie when Sunday school was over.

"Yeah, we would have won easily," Janie sighed. The girls walked slowly down the hallway, their heads drooping.

"Guess we showed you!" Joshua Barton ran up behind Alex and Janie and shouted in their ears.

"Be quiet, Joshua!" Janie retorted.

"Yeah, go away!" Alex added.

"Aw, they're sore losers! Look at the sore losers!" Joshua pranced down the hall with a group of boys.

Alex stuck her tongue out at his back. "Some day I'd like to clobber that kid," she muttered.

"Well, don't do it today," Janie advised her friend. "I think we've had enough trouble for one weekend." Alex nodded her agreement.

For the next few days, Alex fumed about losing the Easter basket contest. Joshua did not make it any easier. He teased the girls endlessly.

"This has been the worst time of my life," Alex told Janie as they trudged home from school.

"Yeah," Janie agreed. "At least school is over and we don't have to see Joshua Barton until after Easter vacation.

"Right," agreed Alex. "That is a relief."

"I'm glad this Sunday is Easter," Janie went on. "Maybe soon we can forget about Easter basket contests.

"Yeah," replied Alex. "Easter baskets have nothing to do with Jesus rising from the dead. That's what Easter is all about."

"You're right," Janie agreed. "Happy Easter, Alex!" she cried as she ran through the back gate to her house.

"Happy Easter, Janie!" Alex called. after her friend.

Easter morning came and Alex awoke suddenly. She thought she had heard a strange noise in her bedroom. Sitting up, Alex sleepily looked around the room. Everything seemed in order. T-Bone lay sound asleep at the foot of her bed. Maybe the noise had been T-Bone stirring in his sleep.

Alex lay back down. She did not want to get up yet. It was too early.

A sudden high-pitched kind of squeak, followed by a "scratch-scratch" jolted Alex upright again.

What was that? This time, T-Bone opened one eye and stared at her from the end of the bed.

"Did you hear that?" Alex asked the dog.

"WOOF!" came T-Bone's reply. He jumped off the bed and lay down beside it, sticking his nose under the bed.

"Is there something under the bed?" Alex asked the dog.

"WOOF! WOOF!" T-Bone answered,

not moving from his position.

Alex, very carefully, got down off the bed. Staying well behind T-Bone, Alex bent down and peered under the bed.

A fairly large shoe box lay under the bed, close to Alex's side. Holes had been punched all along the side of the box. A big blue bow was wrapped around the box. A little card dangled from the bow.

Alex scooted up to the box and read the card. It said, "Happy Easter, Alex!"

"Look at this, T-Bone," said Alex excitedly. "We got an Easter box instead of an Easter basket."

"WOOF!" answered the dog.

"Well, what do you think is in it?" Alex asked the dog. She picked up the box and almost dropped it when something moved inside.

"There's something alive in there," Alex told T-Bone. "Stand back."

The big dog sniffed the box and wagged his tail. He looked as if he already knew what was in it. Alex, however, could not tell what was in the box by sniffing it. She very cautiously opened the lid and peeked inside.

"Ooooohhhhh!" Alex squealed in delight. Huddled in one corner of the box was a little, gray kitten. It was Tuna!

"Brussels sprouts!" Alex cried, taking the kitten in her arms. "I didn't think I'd ever get to keep you."

"Happy Easter, Alex!" her parents suddenly called from the doorway. They had been watching her all along.

"Oh, Mom! Dad!" Alex cried. "Thank you for letting me have Tuna!"

"You're welcome, honey," answered her parents.

"I didn't think you would ever let me have her after all the trouble I caused last week," said Alex.

"We forgive you," Mother smiled.

"Just like Jesus, our Savior, forgave us all when He rose from the dead so many years ago," Father added.

"Yeah, on the very first Easter," said

Alex. She snuggled the kitten in one arm and put her other arm around T-Bone. Smiling up at her parents, Alex prayed, "Thank You, Lord Jesus, for being our Savior, and thank You for giving me such a neat family. Help me to walk with You always and to become one of Your best friends."

Amen.